little Miss Giggles

by Roger Hargreaves

PSS!
PRICE STERN SLOAN

Can you giggle and eat cornflakes at the same time?

Little Miss Giggles could!

Do you giggle while you sleep?

Little Miss Giggles did!

Can you giggle while you brush your teeth?

Little Miss Giggles could!

She was the giggliest girl in the world, and she lived in Chuckle Cottage.

But one terrible day last summer—you'll never guess what happened.

She lost her giggle!

Just like that!

Gone!

She had woken up giggling.

As usual.

She had giggled her way down the stairs.

As usual.

And she had giggled while she was having breakfast.

As usual!

But while she was out walking in the woods around Chuckle Cottage she realized that she wasn't giggling.

She stopped walking.

That's odd, she thought.

Now, *ordinarily*, she would have giggled to herself.

But not today.

She tried to giggle.

Nothing happened!

She tried again.

Nothing happened again!

Oh, dear, she thought miserably.

And, as she walked along, a little tear trickled down her cheek.

She met Mr. Happy, who was out for his usual morning stroll.

"Hello, Little Miss Giggles," he laughed. "And how are you today?"

But then he noticed her sad little face.

"What's wrong?" he asked, anxiously. "You're the happiest person I know!"

He paused.

"Next to myself of course," he added hastily.

"I've lost my giggle," she explained miserably.

"Lost your giggle?" he asked, befuddled.

Mr. Happy scratched his head.

"Hmm," he said. "Well, we'll just have to find it again, won't we?"

Little Miss Giggles nodded, but not very hopefully.

"Come on," he said, and taking her by the hand, he took her off to see Mr. Funny.

"There's nobody like Mr. Funny for a giggle," Mr. Happy said.

But it was no use.

Mr. Funny tried and tried to get her to giggle, chuckle, or even smile, but Little Miss Giggles just couldn't.

"Tell you what," said Mr. Funny. "I'll tell you my very latest joke!"

"Made it up myself," he added modestly. "Very funny!"

He was laughing so hard he could hardly tell the joke. When he had finished, he and Mr. Happy nearly fell over they were laughing so much.

But not Little Miss Giggles!

"It's no use," she sighed. "I'm going to be miserable for the rest of my life, I know I am!"

Then she thought for a moment.

"And I'll have to change my name," she sobbed.

And she started to cry again.

Big fat tears!

Oh dear!

So Mr. Happy took her to see Mr. Topsy Turvy to ask his advice.

"Morning good," he said cheerfully. Then he caught sight of Little Miss Giggles's sad face.

"Matter the what's?" he asked.
(He always spoke back to front!)

Mr. Happy explained what had happened.

"Dear oh!" Mr. Topsy Turvy exclaimed.

Then he thought.

"Doctor," he said. *"Doctor the see to her take!"*

"That's a good idea," said Mr. Happy, and took her right away to see Doctor Make-you-well.

Mr. Happy told the doctor all about Little Miss Giggles's lack of giggle.

"Hmm," he said. "Stick out your tongue!"

"Not you, you silly billy!" he said to Mr. Happy.

Little Miss Giggles stuck out her tongue.

"Looks all right to me," said Doctor Make-you-well. "Open your mouth!"

Doctor Make-you-well peered inside.

"Hmm," he said again. "You're right! Not a giggle in sight!"

"I'm sorry," he added, "but there's nothing I can do for you. You'll just have to wait for your giggle to come back!"

Poor Little Miss Giggles!

Mr. Happy took her home, and by this time even he was not his cheerful self.

What a sorry sight!

Don't you think?

"Why don't you try to giggle?" he said hopefully.

Little Miss Giggles opened her mouth.

"Ha ha ha," she said unhappily.

"Hee hee hee," she said miserably.

"Ho ho ho," she added mournfully.

It was no use.

No use at all!

"I'm sorry I can't help," said Mr. Happy as they reached the garden gate of Chuckle Cottage.

And as Little Miss Giggles went sadly through her front door, Mr. Happy went home. To think.

The IDEA came to him while he was having lunch.

He rubbed his hands with glee.

"Tee hee," he chortled to himself.

And later that afternoon, he knocked on the front door of Chuckle Cottage.

"Who's there?" asked a sad little voice.

"It's me," called out Mr. Happy. "I have a present for you!"

Little Miss Giggles, looking absolutely miserable,
opened the door.

"Here you are," said Mr. Happy, and handed
her a large box.

On top of the box, in large letters, it said:

1 GIGGLE
MEDIUM SIZE
THIS SIDE UP
HANDLE WITH CARE

Little Miss Giggles looked at the box in amazement.

"What is it?" she asked.

"What it says it is," laughed Mr. Happy.
"You lost your giggle, so I got you another one!"

"That giggle cost me a lot of money," he added.

Little Miss Giggles opened the box.

"But there's nothing in it," she exclaimed.

"Of course not," said Mr. Happy. "Giggles are invisible!"

"But that's absolutely ridiculous," said Little Miss Giggles.

"Is it?" chuckled Mr. Happy.

"Of course it is!" she giggled.

She giggled!

She GIGGLED!!